Mike Yamada

COOL CAT VERSUS TOP DOG

First published in Great Britain in 2016 by Frances Lincoln Children's Books,
74-77 White Lion Street, London N1 9PF
www.franceslincoln.com

A catalogue record for this book is available from the British Library.

Hardback ISBN 978-1-84780-738-0
Paperback ISBN 978-1-84780-739-7

Illustrated digitally

Designed by Mike Jolley
Edited by Katie Cotton and Jenny Broom

Printed in China

9 8 7 6 5 4 3 2 1

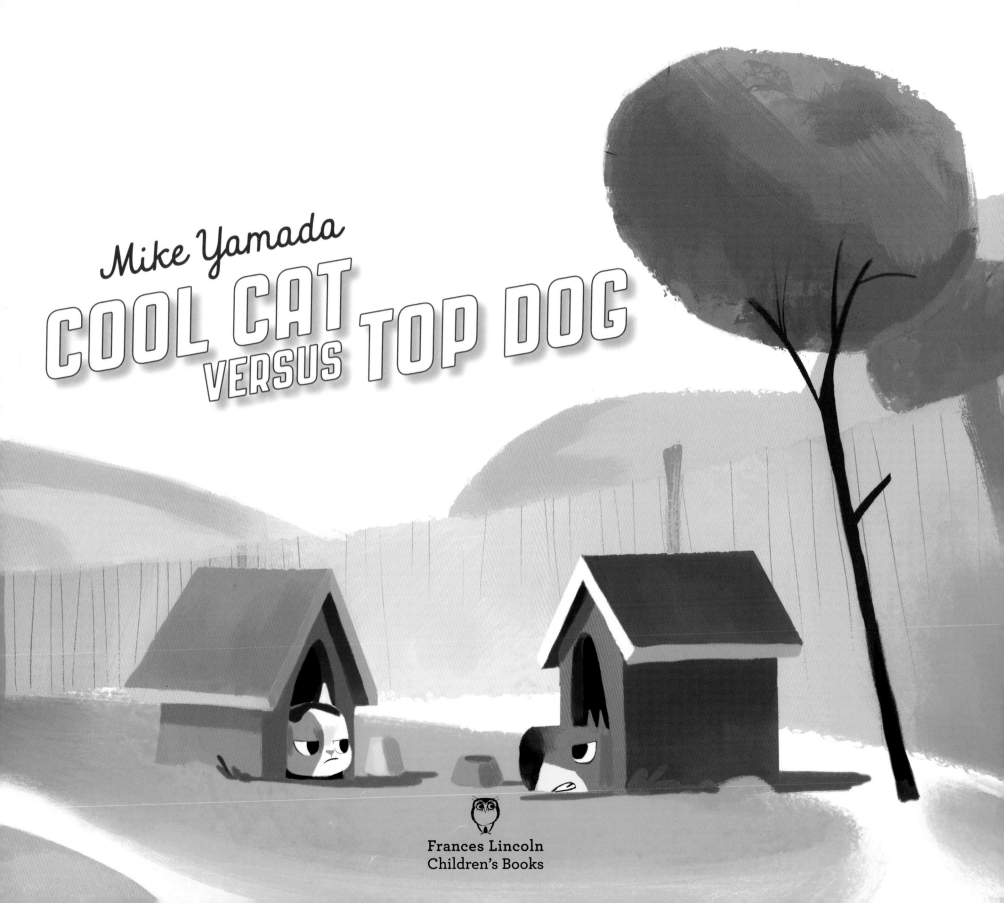

Mike Yamada

COOL CAT VERSUS TOP DOG

Frances Lincoln
Children's Books

In a small town,

in a small house,

lived a small boy,

and his two pets,

Cool Cat and Top Dog.
They would fight over
the smallest thing.

In fact, they
fought like — well,
like cat and dog...

And at the top of the list of things they fought over was...

PET QUEST

~~DOG~~   ~~DOG~~   CAT

~~CAT~~   ~~CAT~~   ~~DOG~~

~~DOG~~   DOG   ~~CAT~~

~~CAT~~   ~~DOG~~

~~DOG~~   ~~CAT~~

~~CAT~~

This high-speed, top-secret, pet-only race had only one winner every year... Cool Cat or Top Dog.

Top Dog had won last time by a whisker, and he just loved to rub his victory in.

Cool Cat spent the year scheming her revenge, while Top Dog was determined to hold onto the prized Pet Quest Cup. Down in their bunkers, the pair tinkered and tweaked their race cars to perfection, until finally...

The night of Pet Quest arrived.
The pets took their places —
Cool Cat and Buck Thumper up front,
with Top Dog just behind. They
revved their engines anxiously
waiting for Fox to shout,

3, 2, 1...

GO!

And they were off!

Top Dog made a
flying start,
leaving Cool Cat
in the dust.

But Cool Cat had a plan.

"It's a dog-eat-dog world!" she shouted as she fired treats from her BONE BAZOOKA. She was sure this would send Top Dog into a spin.

And sure enough...

Top Dog couldn't resist.

Cool Cat raced ahead, joining Buck Thumper in the leader's pack.

"You dirty dog!" yelled Cool Cat as her rival overtook.

And Top Dog's foul
play didn't end there.

Lining himself up
in front of Cool Cat,
he deployed the
POOPER SHOOTER.

This time, Cool Cat was ready for him.

She scooped the poop and threw it in the bin, muttering to herself, "Time for you to do the dog work!"

Then she attached a lead to Top Dog's car, keeping close behind.

Tethered together, and way in front, Top Dog and Cool Cat sped into the final part of the course.

As the finishing line came into sight, Cool Cat chose her moment to pounce.

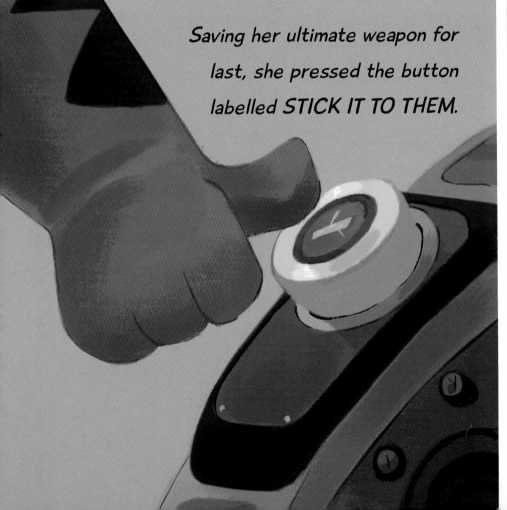

Saving her ultimate weapon for last, she pressed the button labelled STICK IT TO THEM.

A mouth-watering stick flew out of Cool Cat's cannon...

sending Top Dog off course at the vital moment, clearing the way for victory!

But as the frenzied Top Dog leapt to catch it, Cool Cat failed to disconnect the lead and the two cars careered out of control.

Landing in a heap on the floor,
they heard Buck Thumper yell,
"Watch out y'all! It's raining cats and dogs!"
as he sped past them — into the lead!

It was a disaster.

Top Dog's tyres
were punctured
and Cool Cat's engine
was damaged beyond repair.
Neither of them could possibly win now.

As they watched Buck Thumper hurtle towards the finishing line, Top Dog turned to Cool Cat.

"We can't let Big Ears take that cup from us. It belongs to you and me!"

"Let's take my wheels and put them on your car!" said Cool Cat.
"That way we may stand a chance."

So, working as a team,
the pair got Top Dog's car back on the road
and hopped in together.

With Cool Cat at the wheel...

inch by inch they made ground
on Buck Thumper...

and just as the
finishing line
approached...

They crossed the line in first place!
They had won Pet Quest – **together.**